Discard

DATE DUE

DEC 18 2009			
DEC 18 2009			
JAN 27 2010			
JAN 03 2011			
FEB 24 2011			
MAR 14 2011			
MAR 03 2012			
MAY 27 2014			

362.29 Lit

Littell, Mary Ann
Speed and methamphetamine drug dangers

BLACK MOUNTAIN MIDDLE SCHOOL

Discard

Mary Ann Littell

BLACK MOUNTAIN MIDDLE SCHOOL
9353 Oviedo Street
San Diego, CA 92129-2198

Enslow Publishers, Inc.

40 Industrial Road	PO Box 38
Box 398	Aldershot
Berkeley Heights, NJ 07922	Hants GU12 6BP
USA	UK

http://www.enslow.com

Copyright © 1999 by Enslow Publishers, Inc.

All rights reserved.

No part of this book may be reproduced by any means without the written permission of the publisher.

Library of Congress Cataloging-in-Publication Data

Littell, Mary Ann.
    Speed and methamphetamine drug dangers / Mary Ann Littell.
      p. cm. — (Drug dangers)
    Includes bibliographical references and index.
    Summary: Examines the dangers associated with the use of methamphetamines, discussing both medical and legal aspects.
    ISBN 0-7660-1157-7
    1. Amphetamine abuse—United States—Prevention—Juvenile literature. 2. Methamphetamine—Juvenile literature.
[1. Methamphetamine. 2. Amphetamines. 3. Drug abuse.]
I. Title. II. Series.
HV5822.A5L58   1999
362.29'9—dc21   99-10723
                                                                              CIP

Printed in the United States of America

10 9 8 7 6 5 4 3 2 1

To Our Readers:
All Internet addresses in this book were active and appropriate when we went to press. Any comments or suggestions can be sent by e-mail to Comments@enslow.com or to the address on the back cover.

Photo Credits: © Copyright 1997, 1996 T/Maker Company, pp. 35, 56; Corel Corporation, pp. 6, 9, 16, 17, 27, 33, 47; Corbis Digital Stock, pp. 28, 30, 41, 53, 55; Enslow Publishers, Inc., pp. 10, 13, 18, 22; National Archives, p. 38.

Cover Photo: Images © 1995 Photo Disc, Inc.

contents

1 Methamphetamine—
A Persistent Problem 5

2 About Methamphetamine 12

3 Using Methamphetamine 24

4 Where Methamphetamine
Came From 32

5 Fighting Abuse 43

6 Avoiding Drugs 51

Chapter Notes 58

Where to Write for Help 62

Further Reading 63

Index 64

Titles in the **Drug Dangers** series:

Alcohol Drug Dangers
ISBN 0-7660-1159-3

Crack and Cocaine Drug Dangers
ISBN 0-7660-1155-0

Diet Pill Drug Dangers
ISBN 0-7660-1158-5

Heroin Drug Dangers
ISBN 0-7660-1156-9

Inhalant Drug Dangers
ISBN 0-7660-1153-4

Marijuana Drug Dangers
ISBN 0-7660-1214-X

Speed and Methamphetamine Drug Dangers
ISBN 0-7660-1157-7

Steroid Drug Dangers
ISBN 0-7660-1154-2

one

Methamphetamine— A Persistent Problem

For most kids, Christmas and the days that follow are some of the best days of the year. But for three young children in Aguanga, California, the day after Christmas was the worst day of their lives. They died in a horrible fire—a fire that did not have to happen.

Early on the morning of December 26, 1995, people in Aguanga heard an enormous explosion. Frightened neighbors came running to find a large mobile home burning to the ground. Flames shot toward the sky, and dense black smoke was everywhere. Kathy James lived in the mobile home with her four young children. She and her seven-year-old son, Jimmy, managed to escape. But her other three children were trapped in the trailer. Neighbors could hear them screaming for help.

Kathy James was seriously burned, and she

Speed and Methamphetamine Drug Dangers

The chemicals used to make methamphetamine are quite explosive. Kathy Jones accidentally set her mobile home on fire while trying to make a batch of methamphetamine.

seemed out of it. She insisted that she did not need help, and she did not show much concern for her three children who were still trapped in the fire. She did not even want anyone to call the police or the fire department. When police and firefighters finally did arrive, Kathy wandered off.

The fire was eventually put out, but it was too late for the three children. Investigators soon learned, however, the reason Kathy James had been acting so strangely and why she disappeared. The fire was caused by her "cooking" a batch of methamphetamine in her kitchen. The chemicals in this drug are very explosive. Police assumed that some of them spilled onto the stove and exploded.[1]

Methamphetamine—A Persistent Problem

Few drugs are strong enough to kill a mother's love for her children. Methamphetamine is one of them.

The Curse of Methamphetamine

Methamphetamine is nothing new. It has been a problem for many years in California, where it originally came from, and in the Southwest. It has moved across the United States into the Midwest, the South, and beyond. Its reach is far—from the backwoods barns of Missouri to American Indian reservations in the Dakotas and to meat-packing factories in Iowa and Nebraska.[2]

"We're in the middle of a meth epidemic," said one drug enforcement officer. "It's from high school all the way up to the age people should know better."[3]

The chart below shows the increase in methamphetamine use over a three-year period.

In Des Moines, Iowa's largest city, police recently seized $4.5 million worth of methamphetamine. In Polk County, Iowa, more people were arrested for drugs than

Methamphetamine Use 1994–1996

Year	Number of People Who Have Tried Methamphetamine
1994	3.8 million
1995	4.7 million
1996	4.9 million

Taken from the 1996 National Household Survey on Drug Abuse.

for drunk driving—and 65 percent of the drug arrests were for methamphetamine.[4]

"Meth takes control of people who use it," said Steve Johnson, the prosecutor in Jasper County, Iowa. "We're pretty frustrated and don't know exactly what to do to get it under control."[5]

Why is methamphetamine catching on in such a big way? Nobody knows for sure. Some drug experts call it the poor man's cocaine. Like cocaine, it can be smoked, sniffed, or injected with a needle. It is much cheaper than cocaine, however, and keeps a user going for days. Users do not feel the need to eat or sleep. It gives them what appears to be endless energy.

The drug is especially popular among people who work long hours in factories and on assembly lines. A worker on methamphetamine can put in a lot of overtime and not feel tired and stressed out. Maybe that is why it appeals to so many.[6]

"Methamphetamine is often used by blue-collar workers who feel under pressure to perform at a fast pace for long periods," says Dr. Michael Abrams, a drug counselor. "And at first, it works. It turns you into a wonder person. You can do everything—for a while."[7]

Another reason for methamphetamine's popularity may be the fact that it is easy to take. You do not need needles. You can get high snorting or sniffing it.

Methamphetamine is also fairly easy to make. The process does not require a great deal of equipment. Methamphetamine can be cooked up right in someone's garage or kitchen. One police officer said, "The methamphetamine trade is different from any other drug trade. Instead of going to some dark corner of a city, you

Methamphetamine—A Persistent Problem

Methamphetamine users do not feel the need to eat or sleep. As a result, it is especially popular among people who work long hours in factories and on assembly lines.

might be able to get some from your coworker, or your neighbor."[8]

Those people who think methamphetamine is a "safe" drug better think again, however. "It is the most addictive drug known to man," said Dr. Abrams. "A person addicted to it looks and acts just like a paranoid schizophrenic. You can't tell the difference."[9] Schizophrenia is a serious mental illness that has traumatic effects on personality. People with this illness have trouble relating to others and often feel that everyone is against them.

Steve Johnson agrees. He calls methamphetamine users "self-induced mentally ill." This means that users exhibit some of the same symptoms as a mentally ill person, but they have brought on these symptoms by using methamphetamine.

What the Future Holds

Methamphetamine abuse has created serious problems all across the country. However, law enforcement officials believe they are getting a handle on methamphetamine use. They are also getting tough with users.

New laws are making it harder to manufacture and sell the drug. The Comprehensive Methamphetamine Control Act has restricted the sale of chemicals used to

Much of the methamphetamine used in the United States comes from California. It is close to Mexico, which is where many of the chemicals used to make methamphetamine are widely available.

Methamphetamine—A Persistent Problem

make methamphetamine. California has been identified by the Drug Enforcement Agency (DEA) as a source for methamphetamine. Much of the methamphetamine used in the United States comes from California. The state has hundreds of labs where the drug is made. It is also close to Mexico, which is where many of the chemicals for making methamphetamine are widely available. This "Mexican Connection" has made the drug widely available in the West. The United States government is looking at ways to stop the sale of chemicals from Mexico.[10]

Methamphetamine is also a major problem in the Midwest. The state of Iowa has increased drug testing of people on the job in an effort to get methamphetamine out of circulation. Since then, the use of meth at work seems to be decreasing. The state has also passed zero tolerance laws that make it illegal to use even small amounts of the drug. But law enforcement and drug officers know they still have a long way to go. "I am hopeful that we are starting to make a difference," said Johnson. "But this drug gets such a hold on people that it is hard to make them change their behavior. I have never seen anyone kick it on their own, because they wanted to."[11]

One mother's story shows how strong a hold methamphetamine has on its users. Her son wrote to her from prison, where he was serving a few years' time for methamphetamine use. His letter said: "Mom, I hate it here. I can't wait to get out. And when I do, I'm going right back to meth."[12]

two

About Methamphetamine

Imagine a drug that produces a high lasting for hours—or even days. It is cheap to produce. Most of the ingredients can be bought right at the corner drugstore. With some laboratory equipment, the drug can be made in a basement or garage in only a few hours. And the drugmaker does not need a degree in chemistry.

To the drug user, this sounds like a dream come true. But to law enforcement agents, it is their worst nightmare come true. The drug in question is methamphetamine—also called speed, meth, crank, or ice. The DEA is calling it the most dangerous substance to hit the streets during the past thirty-five years.

Methamphetamine used to be known as a bikers' drug, because it was popular with motorcycle gangs. It was most often found in California and the Southwest. Now, however, its

About Methamphetamine

use has spread across the United States, and the drug has become popular with many groups of people. They choose it because it is cheap and gives a long-lasting, intense high. For only twenty-five dollars, a user can be high for up to four days.[1]

Methamphetamine is creeping across the country. It is found in the Midwest, on the West Coast, and parts of the East Coast. Most users are white and come from rural areas or the suburbs.[2] Most methamphetamine is made in California. "What Colombia is to cocaine, California is to methamphetamine," said Bill Mitchell of the DEA office in San Francisco.[3]

One way experts measure methamphetamine use is by looking at how many labs have been shut down. The following map shows where labs were seized and shut down in 1995. California, the unofficial home of meth,

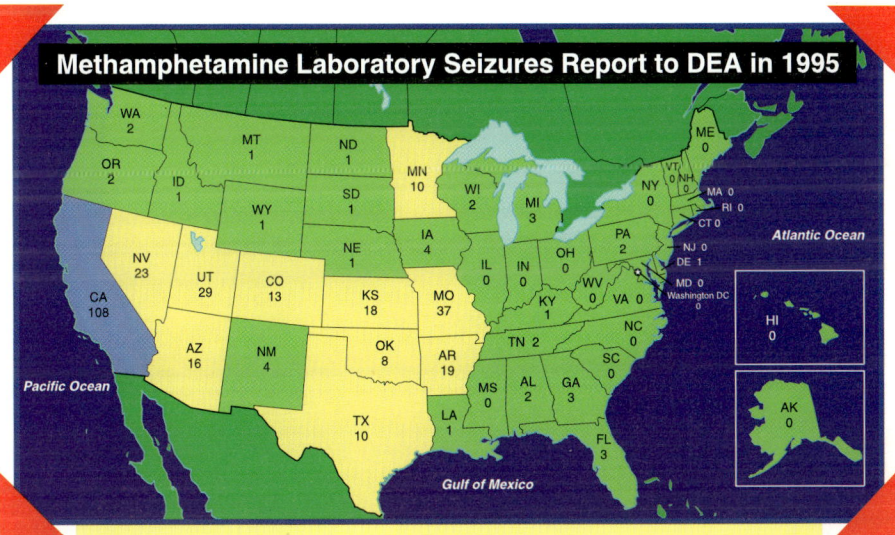

The Drug Enforcement Agency has shut down hundreds of illegal methamphetamine labs in the last several years, but the labs just keep popping up again.

leads the list with 108 labs. But meth manufacture is a problem for many Midwestern states as well.

In 1996 the DEA shut down 303 meth labs in the Midwest alone—almost one per day. Of those 303, the majority—250—were in the state of Missouri. Ninety percent of the drug cases in Kansas City, Missouri, are methamphetamine related. The United States attorney of Missouri, Stephen Hill, estimates that between four hundred and five hundred labs were shut down in Missouri in 1997.[4]

Drug agents are alarmed by the way methamphetamine use is spreading across the country to the eastern and southern states. "They haven't seen much of this in the East Coast," said a drug rehabilitation counselor in Iowa. "But it's coming."[5]

The rise in methamphetamine on the West Coast has law enforcement officers concerned about the drug's spreading to other parts of the country. In 1996 the DEA held a conference to discuss the problem and find ways to fight methamphetamine use. To follow up, the White House Office of National Drug Control Policy held another conference in May 1997 in Omaha, Nebraska. The purpose of that conference was to gather new information on the methamphetamine problem and get input from experts on how to reduce the spread of the drug.

Meth Equals Death

From 1992 to 1994 deaths related to methamphetamine increased by 145 percent. The chart on the following page shows the increase in methamphetamine-related deaths in Phoenix, Arizona, and Los Angeles, California, two cities that have been hard hit by methamphetamine abuse.

Methamphetamine-Related Deaths

City	1992	1994
Phoenix	20	122
Los Angeles	68	219

Methamphetamine is also responsible for many emergency room visits among users. From 1992 to 1994 methamphetamine-related emergency room visits in Los Angeles, California, increased by 71 percent. During that time, it was also the number one cause of drug overdoses in San Diego, California.[6] Across the country, the Drug Abuse Warning Network estimates that methamphetamine-related emergency room visits increased 346 percent from 1991 to 1995.[7]

The Monitoring the Future Survey is a yearly study of drug use among young people in the United States. It is sometimes referred to as the High School Senior Survey, because each year many high school seniors are surveyed. However, it also surveys eighth- and tenth-grade students.

According to the most recent survey, methamphetamine use is on the rise among young people. In 1990, 2.7 percent of high school seniors reported using crystal methamphetamine, or "ice." In 1994 that figure had climbed to 3.4 percent of high school seniors. And in 1996 that figure rose even further to 4.4 percent of seniors.[8] Although this number is low, use is increasing. Many experts compare the effects of methamphetamine

Speed and Methamphetamine Drug Dangers

Los Angeles, California, (shown here) has been hard hit by methamphetamine abuse.

to those of crack cocaine, another very dangerous drug. Both are burned and the fumes inhaled. Both are stimulants. And use of both leads to dependence or addiction.[9]

Researchers are also worried about the large numbers of women who are experimenting with methamphetamine. Researchers from the National Institute of Justice reported that methamphetamine users in their twenties are more likely to be women than men. In eight western cities, among drug users who were arrested, more women than men were found to have used methamphetamine. "Women are testing positive for meth at a higher rate than men," said one government official. "That's the first time we've seen that with any drug."[10]

This increase in use among women is part of a larger picture that shows an increase in all kinds of drug use

About Methamphetamine

among women. A recent report indicated that 3.1 million American women regularly used illegal drugs. Among teenagers, girls and boys were equally likely to have used drugs.[11] This is a shift from the past trend of more drug use among boys than girls.

One reason for methamphetamine's popularity among women may be because it causes people to lose weight very quickly. In our society thin is in, particularly among teenage girls and young women. Many girls and women think that they need to be extremely thin to look good.

During puberty, girls gain an average of twenty to thirty pounds. Though this weight gain is entirely normal, most teens are unprepared for it. Most health classes talk about body changes during puberty, but do not prepare

Methamphetamine's popularity among young women may be due to the fact that it causes weight loss. Many young girls and women mistakenly think that they need to be as thin as a fashion model to look good.

girls for this weight gain. As a result, many girls think they are getting "fat." They turn to unhealthy dieting as a way to stay thin, or they experiment with dangerous drugs—including methamphetamine, which has a history of use as a weight loss drug.

Mother's Little Helper

Were the Rolling Stones describing methamphetamine in "Mother's Little Helper," their famous song of the 1960s? Nobody knows for sure. But one mother described methamphetamine in just that way. It gave her the buzz of one thousand cups of coffee. It kept her going when she was tired. In fact, she did not sleep at all when she was high. She had enough energy to clean her house and

Methamphetamine's effects have been compared to the buzz of one thousand cups of coffee.

About Methamphetamine

take care of her newborn baby. And methamphetamine kept her thin.

Unfortunately, she got so hooked on the drug that it ruined her life. Her marriage fell apart, she lost her son, and she had to go through rehab four times before she could give up meth. "I was a garbage pit," she said.[12]

Methamphetamine's Effect on Behavior

Methamphetamine gives a high that kicks in right away. The first feeling is one of great energy. Any feelings of tiredness go away. The word *euphoria* is often used to describe a methamphetamine high. The user feels a sense of excitement and well-being. A user may believe he or she can do anything. This "superman syndrome" can lead a meth user to do dangerous things.[13]

The chart on the following page shows the many stages of abuse.

Tweaking

People who are hooked on methamphetamine know how to avoid the crash. They simply take more of the drug. However, each additional rush becomes less intense and pleasurable. It takes more and more meth to maintain the normal feeling. This situation leads to a violent, paranoid state of mind that is called tweaking.

Tweakers can be dangerous. Perhaps they have not slept or eaten in days. Their behavior can be unpredictable and negative. They crave more and more of the drug. But even very large amounts of the drug will not bring them back to that original euphoric high. As a result, tweakers get angry and frustrated.

If you look closely, you will see the eyes of

Stages of Methamphetamine Abuse

Stage	Effects of Stage
Rush (5–30 minutes)	Strong feelings of pleasure. The heart races and blood pressure rises.
High (4–16 hours)	The abuser feels smart, aggressive. Can be very argumentative.
Binge (3–15 days)	The abuser stays high as long as possible. Becomes hyperactive, both mentally and physically. Does not require much sleep.
Tweaking	The most dangerous stage of the cycle. (Described in detail in this chapter.)
Crash (1–3 days)	The user comes down from the high. Has very low energy and sleeps a lot.
Stable, or holding (2–14 days)	The abuser is not high at all, but is not back to normal. Still feels angry, on edge.
Withdrawal (30–90 days)	Abuser is depressed. Craves the drug. May become suicidal. Taking the drug during this period gives an immediate high and stops feelings of depression, making it hard to kick the habit.

Taken from Methamphetamine Fact Sheet, Prevline, March 26, 1998.

methamphetamine users darting much faster than normal. They may talk loudly and energetically. Their movements can be fast and jerky. They often focus on tiny details for hours, taking something apart and then putting it back together over and over.

The anger and paranoia of methamphetamine users can cause them to commit terrible crimes. In New Mexico, a man who was high on methamphetamine and had also been drinking alcohol cut his fourteen-year-old son's head off, raced down a busy highway in his car, and finally threw the head out of his car window.[14]

About Methamphetamine

In another incident, an Idaho woman high on meth attacked her family with a rake when they tried to convince her to go into rehab. She swung the handle full force into her husband's abdomen, damaging his kidneys. Then she turned the rake on her mother, scratching her so severely that she was badly scarred. The woman with the rake had been a long-time methamphetamine abuser.[15]

Women who use methamphetamine may become prone to other types of abusive, violent behavior. Some experts believe that these women may be more likely to abuse their children or pass their addiction on to them. In 1996 a hospital in Sacramento, California, reported that there were more babies being born addicted to methamphetamines than to crack. "This drug is one of the few things powerful enough to shatter a mother's love for her child," said General Barry McCaffrey, director of drug policy under President Clinton.[16]

A Health Hazard to Everyone

As if the news about methamphetamine was not bad enough, there is still more important evidence of methamphetamine's dangers. Methamphetamine is not just harmful to individuals. It also harms the environment.

Many dangerous, even poisonous substances are used to manufacture the drug. These substances pollute soil and water. All manufacturers must obey certain laws when disposing of chemical wastes. Drugmakers are already breaking antidrug laws. They do not care about laws protecting the environment. They just want to make their product and make a profit. When they are finished producing methamphetamine, they are left with harmful by-products. (By-products are anything that is left over

Many dangerous, even poisonous, substances are used to make methamphetamine. After methamphetamine is made, the poisonous material that is left is often dumped without regard for safety.

when a substance is manufactured.) The drugmakers dump these poisonous by-products wherever they can.

Cleaning up these chemicals costs taxpayers millions of dollars a year. And these chemicals may have serious effects on the future health of people everywhere. That is one of the reasons that President Clinton signed a bill to control the spread of methamphetamine.[17]

Some of the ingredients used in methamphetamine are so dangerous that they can harm anyone who simply comes near them. One police officer in Independence, Missouri, suffered a badly burned throat when he breathed fumes from an illegal meth lab. As a result, all members of his antidrug team now wear protective suits and masks when looking into illegal labs.

Illegal labs have many other dangers as well. Methamphetamine makers are not scientists. They do not know proper safety measures. Sometimes they heat the chemicals to very high temperatures, trying to speed up the process. Many illegal labs have blown up as a result. Imagine that you lived next door to someone who made methamphetamine. Your life could be in danger if such an explosion occurred or if toxic chemicals leaked onto your property or into your water supply.

To put a stop to the manufacture of methamphetamine, local government officials in California and Missouri are putting a limit on sales of cold and allergy medicines. (Other states, including Kansas, Arizona, and Minnesota, are considering similar limits.) Many of these medicines contain ingredients that are used to make methamphetamine. For instance, in San Diego it is illegal to buy more than three packages of cold and allergy medicines in a twenty-four hour period. In some Wal-Mart stores, if a customer tries to buy more than three packages of cold medicine at once, the cash register shuts down.

Warner-Lambert, a pharmaceutical company in New Jersey, is working on a chemical that will prevent people from making methamphetamine from cold medicines.[18] The use of methamphetamine—and of all drugs—affects everyone, in both direct and indirect ways.

three

Using Methamphetamine

Growing up can be difficult and stressful. Young people face many pressures. There is pressure to do well in school, to get good grades, and do well in all activities in which they participate. Peer pressure can also be hard to cope with. Teens want to be popular and well liked, to fit in with others. They may feel as if they have to act and dress a certain way to be accepted. The wrong shoes or clothing can spell disaster for a teen's image.

To make matters even more complicated, the body changes as a teen goes through puberty. The body grows taller and develops sexually. For girls, some of these changes include breast development, growth of body hair, and menstruation. For boys, changes at puberty include the growth of body and facial hair and deepening of the voice. These changes can be difficult and confusing.

Using Methamphetamine

Some teens turn to drugs as a way of coping with stress. They may think drugs will help them escape an unhappy home life, problems getting along with friends, or poor grades in school. Some teenagers use drugs because other kids use them, and they want to fit in with a certain crowd. Still others use drugs because they are bored. Drugs do not help fix any of these problems, however. No drug can change who a teen is or help him or her connect with the outside world. Getting high may seem like a way of escaping problems, but it is not.

If problems exist, drugs will not help solve them. And a very strong, mind-altering drug like methamphetamine can actually make problems much worse. Here are a few stories of young people who have abused methamphetamine. For some of these people, using meth was a deadly mistake. Others lived to kick the habit but deeply hurt themselves and their families.

Too Much Dieting

Weight gain is a perfectly normal part of puberty. However, to many teenage girls who are not prepared for them, these extra pounds are unexpected and alarming. Young girls may have learned all about sexual development in family life classes, but nobody told them about the weight gain that is a normal part of puberty.

In our society, thin is in. This rule holds true for girls, but only sometimes for boys. According to research, boys welcome the weight gain that comes with puberty. In fact, in a recent poll, many boys said they wished they would gain a few more pounds, to build bigger muscles.

Girls, on the other hand, do not welcome this extra weight. They do not want muscles and worry that they will be considered fat. Many try binge dieting to lose weight. They starve themselves or eat and then make themselves throw up. Others may turn to methamphetamine, thinking that it will aid in weight loss. One drug counselor said, "It is a concern. It's not something we see all the time, but young women we are seeing have said they've used methamphetamine to lose weight."[1]

An Iowa doctor who treats young drug users said that 10 to 12 percent of middle-school-age girls who think they are overweight have tried methamphetamine. "I see some of them at age fourteen or fifteen, and by then, they've been using [for] a couple of years already."[2]

Methamphetamine users feel as if they do not need much food. They get chemical energy from the drug. It keeps them going for hours. When they do eat, it is usually smaller amounts of food.

Methamphetamine also has many side effects that cause weight loss. People on the drug do not sleep, and they are very alert and energetic. They use up a great deal of energy. Diarrhea and vomiting, other side effects of methamphetamine, also contribute to weight loss.

Someone using methamphetamine to lose weight sees results quickly. People have been known to lose ten pounds or more a week while on the drug. But it is a dangerous, and sometimes deadly, way to lose weight.

As a teenager growing up in Idaho, Amy Jo dreamed of being a ballerina. She turned to methamphetamine to become dancer slim. It was a mistake. She lost thirty-five pounds in one month while on the drug. In just a short time, she fell completely under the spell of methamphetamine. She would stay up all night doing the drug, then sleep until noon. Before too long, she lost her job in a beauty shop.

Using Methamphetamine

Young women who dream of becoming "dancer slim" may make the mistake of resorting to methamphetamine to lose weight.

Amy Jo would call her mother and plead for help. But when her mother tried to help her, Amy Jo would say no. Eventually she was arrested for her methamphetamine use. Her cell mate in jail was nineteen-year old Salena. She had been on a six-week methamphetamine binge. Her weight had dropped to only ninety pounds.

After a few months in prison, the two women committed suicide together. They hanged themselves from bedsheets looped through the prison bars. The two young women were not high when they killed themselves. They had not used methamphetamine since going to prison. But the drug is so strong that months later, they were still under its deadly grip. They felt the symptoms of withdrawal.[3]

Said one Iowa lawyer who is fighting to get methamphetamine off the streets: "The basic message is that meth is a disaster if you get into it. It really is life or meth."[4]

Other Methamphetamine Victims

Weight loss is not the only reason young women use methamphetamine. Lori, a young woman from Oregon, began using the drug as a teenager. She simply wanted to get high. She used so much of it that she became very sick. By the time she was twenty, she had already had a heart attack. "I weighed eighty-six pounds," she said. "Spandex would fall off me. You could smell meth coming out of my pores."

Lori's life revolved around the drug. Unable to work, she depended on welfare. The state of Oregon then changed the rules about welfare, and Lori was told she had to try to get a job. The state would help her by sending her to school.

Methamphetamine abuse can ruin lives. Those who do not die as a result of their habit may end up in jail.

Using Methamphetamine

When Lori refused to show up, her welfare check was reduced. This forced her to go into treatment. She spent a year in rehab and was able to kick the habit. Today, Lori has a good job.[5] Others are not so lucky, however.

Girls are not the only ones who turn to methamphetamine. Boys use it, too—with equally bad results. When seventeen-year-old Travis of Waterloo, Iowa, told his parents he was using crank (another word for methamphetamine), they were shocked. His father wanted Travis to go into rehab, but Travis said he could kick the habit on his own.

Unfortunately, like many methamphetamine users, Travis could not stay away from the drug. He lost weight and became angry and abusive. After several fights with his parents, they kicked him out of the house.

A few weeks later, Travis went to a hospital. He felt terribly sick. At first, it seemed as if he had the flu. But then doctors found that it was much worse. Methamphetamine had destroyed Travis's immune system. He developed a serious infection and died.[6]

People who use methamphetamine are a danger to themselves as well as to others. Eleven-year-old Adam from Canton, Georgia, was killed in a car crash in June 1997. Adam's mother was driving, and he was in the backseat. Another car rammed into the back of the Jenkins's car. The driver of the other car, a twenty-one-year-old woman, was high on methamphetamine at the time of the accident.

The driver of the car that caused the accident was sent to prison for thirteen years. But that punishment was not enough for Adam's mother. She asked the judge to be sure that the imprisoned woman did not forget Adam. So the judge ordered the woman to visit Adam's grave

People who use methamphetamine are a danger to themselves as well as to others.

every year on June 10—the anniversary of the crash.[7] Adam was a victim of methamphetamine use, even though he did not use the drug.

Does Someone You Know Use Methamphetamine?

What would you do if someone you knew—a friend, a sister, or a brother—became involved with methamphetamine or any other drug?

Methamphetamine is widely available in many parts of the country. Different kinds of people use it for many reasons. It can be found anywhere—in neighborhoods, schools, public places, on the street, and even in the home.

Many drug users have one important thing in

Using Methamphetamine

common: They do not want anyone to know about their drug use. People who use drugs generally try to keep their use a secret. If their teachers find out, they may be kicked out of school. If their parents find out, they will get in trouble and be punished or grounded. If the police find out, they might be arrested.

What Would You Do?

1. You suspect your older sister is using methamphetamine. She is always worrying about gaining weight. Lately, you notice she has lost a lot of weight, and she never seems to sleep. She stays up all night long, listening to music or talking on the phone. What do you tell your parents?

2. Your best friend is acting weird—really hyper. She has started sneaking out of school several times a week, and she is hanging around with a new group of people. Rumor has it these "new friends" use methamphetamine. You asked her if anything was wrong. She said it was none of your business. Now she will not talk to you at all. What should you do?

3. You are in the park with a few of your friends. Some older kids come by and show you a bag of white crystals that look like small ice cubes. They tell you it is "ice" and offer to sell it to you, but you say no. What should you do next?

4. You are at a local sports stadium, attending a basketball game with your family. You go to the bathroom and see a hypodermic needle on the floor. It looks as if it has already been used. What do you do?

four

Where Methamphetamine Came From

Methamphetamine is a drug that affects the brain. It is very much like amphetamine. Both drugs have powerful effects on the central nervous system. However, methamphetamine is stronger than amphetamine.

Though methamphetamine has been in the news quite a bit lately, it is not a new drug. It has been around for many years. During World War II, methamphetamine was used by American soldiers and German soldiers to boost their energy.[1] It was given by injection. This form of methamphetamine was not considered dangerous at all. Soldiers who took the drug needed less sleep, making them more effective in fighting the enemy.

In the 1950s methamphetamine was widely used by college students, athletes, and truck drivers to give them more energy and keep them from getting tired. Back then, methamphetamine

Where Methamphetamine Came From

was taken in pill form. It was a legal drug.[2] People who wanted it simply went to their doctors and asked for prescriptions. Few people taking the drug became seriously addicted. But some did become very dependent on methamphetamine. They got used to feeling energetic. They felt as if they could do anything. Once that happened, methamphetamine was a tough habit to break. During this time, methamphetamine also began to be used as a medicine to help people lose weight. It took away feelings of hunger. People on the drug could go for days without eating.[3]

In the 1960s a new form of methamphetamine became widely available. This form was also injected by needle, but it was much stronger than the methamphetamine used by the military. It was also

During World War II, methamphetamine was used by American and German soldiers to boost their energy. The dangers of use were not yet known.

extremely addictive. People who took it quickly became hooked. To cut back the use of this dangerous drug, the government passed the Controlled Substances Act in 1970. It was now against the law to make or sell methamphetamine.[4]

New laws made methamphetamine much less available. However, people who wanted it could easily find it for sale on the streets. They continued to use it, even though it was illegal. In the 1970s methamphetamine became known as a "biker drug" because of its popularity with motorcycle gangs on the West Coast. They made the drug themselves and sold it.[5] The drug received the nickname "crank" because bikers hid the drug inside their motorcycle's crank case. (The crank case is a steel case containing a motorcycle's gears.)

Methamphetamine has earned its reputation for being a very dangerous drug. Even small amounts of it have strong effects on the brain. In the 1970s one antidrug campaign warned that "speed kills." Speed is another name for methamphetamine.

Today, methamphetamine is still made in illegal laboratories. Making methamphetamine requires some special knowledge of chemistry. However, as one police officer put it, "It doesn't take a brain surgeon."[6] No special equipment is needed, either. Many people set up labs right in their homes and garages. They make small amounts of the drug, sometimes less than a pound at a time. "These guys consume part of the product and sell the rest to their friends," said drug agent Michael P. Shanahan.[7]

One of the main ingredients in methamphetamine is a chemical called ephedrine. A few years ago the government passed laws against selling ephedrine.

Where Methamphetamine Came From

Methamphetamine became known as a biker drug because of its popularity with motorcycle gangs on the West Coast.

They thought this would reduce the supply of methamphetamine. Unfortunately, the new laws did not stop people from making methamphetamine. The drugmakers used other ingredients instead. Now, a chemical called pseudoephedrine is used to make methamphetamine. The word *pseudo* means "fake." Pseudoephedrine is a slightly altered version of ephedrine. It has the same effects on the brain. Pseudoephedrine is found in many legal drugs, including weight loss pills and medicines used for colds and flu. These drugs are sold over the counter in supermarkets and drugstores. Because pseudoephedrine is not an illegal substance and is very easy to find, drugmakers continue to make methamphetamine illegally.

Other ingredients used in making methamphetamine are considered quite dangerous. Lye, rat poison, and even battery acid have been used in making methamphetamine. Other possible ingredients include antifreeze, drain cleaner, and muriatic acid, a strong substance that can dissolve concrete.

Some "cooks" have been known to mix up a batch right in a frying pan on a stove. It has been made in hotels, motels, bathtubs, even the trunks of cars. When methamphetamine is being made, it gives off a powerful smell. Some people compare the smell to that of urine. You can smell it from far away. The odor is a giveaway that methamphetamine is being made. Nothing else smells quite like it.

Because of the smell, many methamphetamine makers move their labs to out-of-the-way, sparsely populated areas, where there are not many people around who might get suspicious. They may go to farms or abandoned buildings to make the drug.

Crank and Ice

All drugs are classified by the government according to how dangerous and addictive they are. Methamphetamine is classified as a Schedule II drug. This term is used to describe drugs with medical properties that are also very likely to be abused and to cause abusers to become addicted. Methamphetamine is in this category, even though its medical use is very limited. It is against the law to manufacture, sell, or use any Schedule II drug.

Methamphetamine comes in different forms. It may be sold as pills, capsules, powder, or chunks. It also has many nicknames. The following chart lists some of the names by which methamphetamine is known.

Where Methamphetamine Came From

Methamphetamine Nicknames

Nickname	Type of Methamphetamine
ice, crystal, glass	crystallized methamphetamine
crank, speed, meth, chalk	called "street methamphetamine" because it is the type most commonly available on the streets, in pills, capsules, or powder

Methamphetamine is usually swallowed or snorted (inhaled through the nose). It can also be injected with a needle or smoked, however. Ice looks just like its name. It is clear or white and comes in chunks, similar to an ice cube. Ice is smoked or injected with a needle. It gives a very intense high. The other forms of methamphetamine can be taken orally, snorted, or injected.

Many people compare methamphetamine to crack cocaine, because both drugs provide an intense high. However, there are many differences between the drugs. Methamphetamine costs much less than crack cocaine and provides a much longer high. When its effects wear off, it leaves the user feeling much more "down."

As harmful as crack is, it cannot compare to the destructive power of methamphetamine, said Dr. Michael Abrams of Broadlawn Medical Center in Des Moines, Iowa. Because of the way the drug's molecules are arranged, methamphetamine is more stimulating to the brain than any other drug. And unlike cocaine, which comes from a plant, methamphetamine is a laboratory-made chemical. "The body has substances

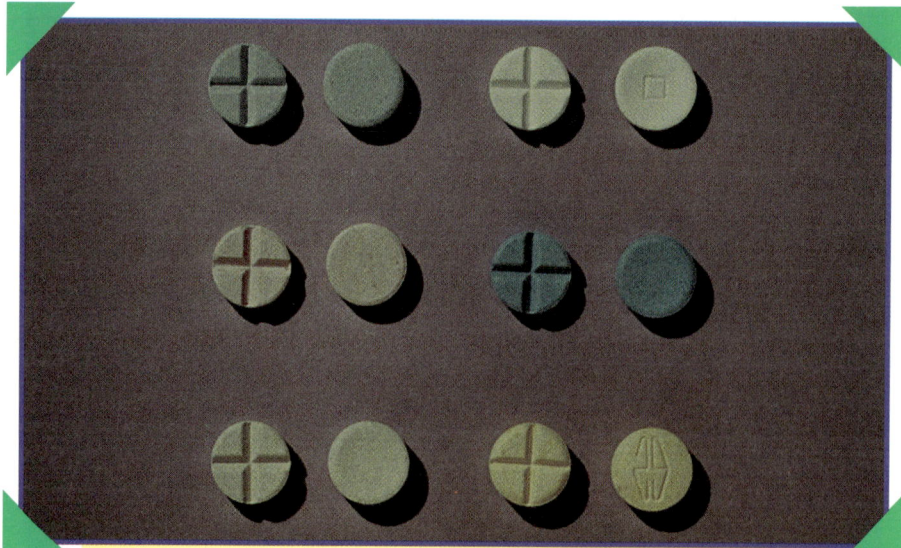

Methamphetamine comes in several different forms. In addition to the pills shown here, methamphetamine may also be sold as capsules, powder, or chunks resembling chunks of ice.

that break down cocaine," said Abrams, "but not methamphetamine."[8]

Methamphetamine's Effects on the Body

Whether it is called crank, speed, or ice—smoked, snorted, or inhaled—methamphetamine is addictive. People who take methamphetamine become hooked on it. They need it to feel normal and want more and more of it.

When ice or crank is smoked or injected, the user feels an intense high right away. This is called a "rush" or "flash." It lasts for only a few minutes. Users describe this feeling as so pleasurable that they want more of the drug.

Swallowing methamphetamine or snorting it also produces a high. The high lasts from eight to twenty-four

Where Methamphetamine Came From

hours. When the user comes down, he or she usually begins craving more of the drug right away.[9]

Methamphetamine stimulates the central nervous system—the brain, spinal cord, and nerves in the human body. Its effects are similar to those of dopamine and adrenaline, two chemicals made by the body. These chemicals make us feel alert and excited. They make our heart beat faster, and raise our blood pressure. We breathe faster, and our brain feels energized. The feeling is similar to the one we get when we exercise.[10]

Methamphetamine affects the body in a similar way but produces a much stronger reaction. When a user takes methamphetamine, it causes a tremendous release of dopamine in the body. Dopamine is the chemical in the body that controls most pleasurable feelings. Some experts call this release a "spike." The bigger the spike, the more intense the high.[11] A user feels hyper and on edge. When the feeling becomes too intense, it makes a user feel angry and fearful. Feelings of nervousness and anxiety are also common.

One of the things that makes methamphetamine so dangerous is the fact that it provides a high that is longer than just about any other drug. While the initial effects of cocaine are gone in twenty to forty minutes, methamphetamine continues to work on the brain for up to twenty-four hours.

Methamphetamine produces both short-term and long-term effects, as seen in the following chart.[12]

In February 1998 the Drug Enforcement Agency held a meeting to discuss the growing problem of methamphetamine abuse. "When I first took office, people talked about methamphetamine use being a problem in the West," said Attorney General Janet Reno.

Methamphetamine's Effects on the Body

Short-Term Effects	Long-Term Effects
acne, sores	depression
aggressive behavior	decreased social life
dry skin	disorganized lifestyle
hallucinations (seeing things that are not there)	permanent hallucinations
hyperactivity	possible brain damage
increased alertness	psychological or mental problems
insomnia (inability to sleep)	serious kidney and lung problems
loss of appetite	violent behavior
paranoia (a feeling that everyone is out to get you)	weight loss
rise in body temperature (as high as 108°F), which can cause brain damage	death

"Let us . . . recognize that it is sweeping across the country. There should be no question in anybody's mind that methamphetamine poses a real and serious threat to the citizens of our nation."[13]

The Cycle of Addiction

When someone becomes addicted to a drug, he or she needs that drug to feel normal. Addictive drugs produce two effects on the body—an initial "feel-good" effect, followed by an unpleasant effect.

Where Methamphetamine Came From

Methamphetamine makes the user feel good while he or she is high. However, when the drug wears off, the user feels down and depressed. The depression is a result of the fact that methamphetamine eventually shuts down the body's natural production of adrenaline and dopamine. The body's natural chemical balance is upset. The user must take more methamphetamine to feel normal again.[14]

Effects on the Mind

Methamphetamine has powerful effects on the mind and the personality. "It gives you a feeling of superiority, like

Methamphetamine makes the user feel good while he or she is high. However, when the effects of the drug wear off, the user can feel down and depressed.

there's nothing you can't do," said a former user who had just completed rehab. "Meth just makes you want to go. You go out to mow the lawn and end up manicuring it."[15]

Personality changes caused by methamphetamine include nervousness and paranoia, the feeling that everyone is against you. Many methamphetamine users lose all interest in their friends and family.

Methamphetamine's Effects

- Aggressiveness
- Anxiety
- Depression
- Disinterest in friends and/or food
- Disturbed sleep
- Excessive talking
- Excessive excitedness
- Feelings of power
- Irritability
- Moodiness
- Nervousness
- Panic

Health Hazards

Those who abuse illegal drugs put their health at risk. Significant health risks come as a result of sharing needles, as many drug users do.

five

Fighting Abuse

When you think of teens and drugs, methamphetamine is probably not the first drug that comes to mind. Even so, it appeals to teens for many reasons. It does not cost much, and just a little produces a high that lasts a long time. It also contributes to weight loss.

Methamphetamine is also extremely addictive. People who use it develop a craving for the drug. They want to use it all the time. It is the first thing they think about in the morning, and the last thing they think about at night. This craving can ruin the lives of many drug users and their families.

Each year, more than one million American families must deal with a drug problem. Some families face the problem and try to solve it. Others avoid the problem and pretend it does not exist. They may not want to think about the fact that their children are using drugs—especially an

Speed and Methamphetamine Drug Dangers

addictive drug like methamphetamine. Sometimes they just ignore the problem and hope it goes away.

Unfortunately, a problem with methamphetamine will not usually go away on its own. "I've been around many people on meth—but I have never seen someone decide to stop using it and kick the habit on their own," said Jasper County attorney Steve Johnson. "Meth users need help—and lots of it."[1]

The first and most important step in finding help is admitting the existence of a drug problem. Unfortunately, most methamphetamine users are unable to do this. They believe there is nothing wrong with using the drug. They think, "I control the drug, it doesn't control me."

Parents, teachers, and friends of a methamphetamine user must know the signs of drug use. The following chart lists some of the most common signs.[2]

It is practically impossible for someone to kick a methamphetamine habit without help. The user should seek help from people who are trained to treat drug addiction. This help is available through many sources.

Addiction

These are a few of the signs of addiction:

- Lying to parents and teachers.
- Being high is everything. It is the most important thing in life.
- Thinking that quitting is easy—but the user can't do it alone.[2]

Treating Addiction

"Curing an addiction is a lifelong process, because it causes permanent changes in the brain—like brain

Fighting Abuse

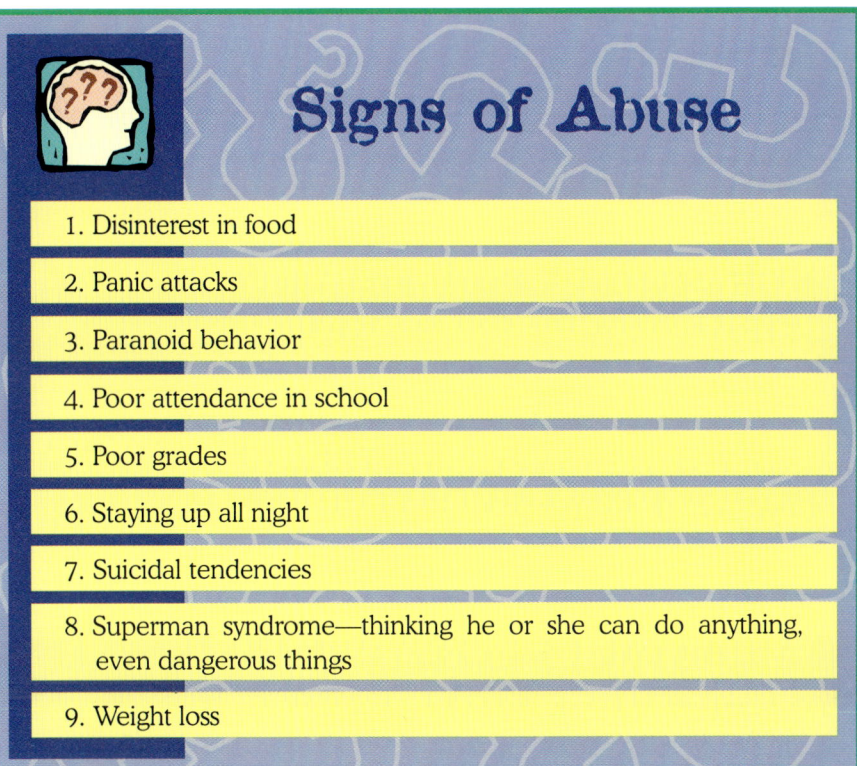

Signs of Abuse

1. Disinterest in food
2. Panic attacks
3. Paranoid behavior
4. Poor attendance in school
5. Poor grades
6. Staying up all night
7. Suicidal tendencies
8. Superman syndrome—thinking he or she can do anything, even dangerous things
9. Weight loss

disease," said Dr. Michael Abrams of the Broadlawn Medical Center in Des Moines, Iowa. "Spend one night with meth, and the rest of your life recovering from it."[3]

Dr. Abrams, who treats many methamphetamine addicts, says more and more young people are trying the drug. "A good deal of it is what we call party use. Teens are at a party, and they take methamphetamine to relax, get social, and feel more accepted. Before too long, they are addicted to the drug. They crave it all the time."[4]

Forty percent of those entering Dr. Abrams's program at Broadlawn Medical Center are methamphetamine users. "Here in Iowa, methamphetamine is so widely available that it's almost like alcohol," he said. "Because

Where to Get Help

Doctors:
Can counsel drug user and refer family to a treatment program

Drug treatment counselors:
Can provide therapy for drug users (counseling to help them stop using drugs)

Hospitals:
Can provide drug treatment counselors

Hotlines:
Can provide information and referrals

Intervention specialists:
Assist families in convincing user to seek treatment

Substance abuse agencies:
Can provide information on drug use and make referrals to drug treatment programs

---

it's out there, many young people are trying it. Most teenagers who come for treatment don't want to be here. They're here because someone, usually their parents, has forced them to come."[5]

At first, parents may ignore their child's methamphetamine use. But methamphetamine causes serious behavior problems. Sooner or later, the user gets out of control. He or she may run wild, do poorly in school, steal things, even wreck a car. Before too long, parents who cannot handle this behavior any more will look for help.

When methamphetamine users come in for treatment, it is usually after they have been using the

Fighting Abuse

drug for a while. They may be having panic attacks or may be seeing things that do not exist. Some want to kill themselves. Heavy users often say they see bugs crawling all over their skin. They can get so upset they may start to pick and scratch at themselves until they are covered with bloody scabs.

The first part of treatment is giving these users medicine to calm them down. It usually takes five to seven days for methamphetamine to leave the system. When they come down from their high, users feel depressed. However, they are still addicted and usually want another hit of the drug right away. They will not remember the panic attacks, the feeling that bugs are crawling on their skin, or any other of methamphetamine's negative side effects.

This lack of recall of methamphetamine's negative

Heavy methamphetamine users often say they see bugs crawling all over their skin.

effects is one of the reasons methamphetamine abuse is so hard to treat. "These users just want to go right back into the addiction circuit," says Dr. Abrams. "They don't learn from their bad experiences. Addicted teenagers don't understand or have scientific knowledge about brain addiction disease. Nor do their parents. They do not realize the brain-craving center now controls the person."[6]

The next phase of treatment is counseling. Users meet with counselors to talk about their drug use. The counselors are trained in helping those who abuse all drugs, not just methamphetamine. Sometimes drug users are grouped together so they can share their experiences. The meetings are called group therapy sessions. Users may also meet one-on-one with counselors to talk about why they use drugs and how to live life without them. For methamphetamine users, one-on-one meetings are usually more effective. Most methamphetamine users do not do well in groups. They are too focused on themselves and their own drug use to listen to other people's problems.[7]

Counselors talk and listen. They try to help drug users know why they use drugs. Some of the reasons teens use drugs are:

- Wanting to fit in and be popular with their peers;
- Coping with an unhappy home life;
- Inability to handle peer pressure.

During treatment, drug users may also learn relaxation techniques, or how to stay calm and feel good without drugs. Many young people use drugs to escape the pain and unhappiness in their lives. Relaxation helps them deal with family or school problems in a positive way. They also watch videos about drug abuse. The goal is to teach drug users that they have a choice about using drugs.

The process of recovering from methamphetamine addiction takes a long time—up to one year or more. Unfortunately, many users do not get the time they need. Many drug users cannot afford to pay for treatment. Their parents' insurance companies or the state government may pay the bill, but only for a few weeks to a month at most. Then the methamphetamine user will most likely go back to using it. "In most cases, they go back on methamphetamine right away," says Steve Johnson.[8]

As a result, only a small number of methamphetamine abusers are actually able to kick the habit. "In our program, about 20 percent of methamphetamine users are helped the first time around. Some of them have to come back two, three, even four times before they are able to override the craving and control the addiction," said Dr. Abrams.[9]

"It really takes a few years for meth addicts to get back to normal," he added. "The effects on the brain are almost like having a stroke. Meth causes abnormalities in the brain cells. Many recovering addicts need daily therapy for a few years."[10]

Drug counseling also involves the families of drug users. Parents meet with counselors to learn how to be most helpful in the recovery process. By staying in control, they can help their children stay off drugs.

Therapeutic Communities

Teens with more serious addiction problems sometimes leave home to live at a drug treatment center. These facilities are called therapeutic communities. Many teens go into these programs after they have been arrested for drug use or other crimes. They are given a choice: Enter a drug treatment program or go to jail. Most choose drug treatment.

There are many residential programs all across the country. Drug users live there for a year or more. They go to school, hold jobs, and meet with counselors. Although many users do not want to leave family and friends to live away from home, sometimes it is necessary. Some drug users want to give up drugs, but their drug-using friends will not let them. Others may have serious family problems that they need to get away from.

With treatment, many methamphetamine users are able to put their lives back together. But it takes time. And there is no guarantee that they will be cured of their addiction.

"In a new survey, 56 percent of teens in the U.S. don't see any risk in taking meth," said Dr. Abrams. "The survey also points out that parents believe their children understand and have knowledge about the risks and dangers of meth, but only 44 percent of kids perceive this risk."[11]

The choice to use methamphetamine or any other drug is up to the individual. The smartest choice is never to use it (or any other illegal drugs) at all. Drug counselors agree: Methamphetamine is definitely a drug to stay away from. Most people have no idea how powerfully it can affect a person. Why take chances?

six

Avoiding Drugs

On October 3, 1996, President Bill Clinton signed a new law into effect called the Comprehensive Methamphetamine Control Act. This law makes it a crime for anyone to have the chemicals and equipment needed to make methamphetamine. It increases the amount of jail time given to those who make or sell methamphetamine.

President Clinton said, "I am particularly pleased we are acting before this epidemic spreads. We have to stop meth before it becomes the crack of the nineties. And this legislation gives us the chance to do it."[1]

Unfortunately, use of methamphetamine is still on the rise. However, drug experts hope that methamphetamine use may be starting to slow down. The Drug Abuse Warning Network (DAWN) collects information on drug-related visits to hospital emergency departments. It is a

Speed and Methamphetamine Drug Dangers

useful way of tracking increases in drug use. Information from the 1996 DAWN survey indicates that methamphetamine-related visits increased by 237 percent between 1990 and 1994, but decreased by 39 percent between 1994 and 1996.[2]

The best way to reduce the use of all drugs, including methamphetamine, is through prevention. If you can prevent people from ever trying drugs, you will avoid the problems caused by drug abuse.

America's war on drugs is having an impact on abuse of some, but not all drugs. It is a sad fact that many young people are still trying drugs. It is up to parents to talk to their kids about the risks of drug use. Schools, churches, synagogues, and community groups also need to spread the message against drugs. Police and other law officers must work hard to keep drugs off the streets.

In a recent survey, 23.5 percent of twelve-year-olds said they knew someone who had used drugs.[3] People who use drugs often try to get others to use them too. This peer pressure can push people into taking drugs they really do not want to try.

Fighting Peer Pressure

Drugs are out there. They are available. They are in schools and in neighborhoods. Because drugs are all around, saying no to them can be difficult especially if friends or classmates are using them. Many young people find it difficult to avoid doing things their friends are doing, even when they know those things are wrong.

Many schools take part in a program called D.A.R.E. The program teaches students of all ages about the risks of drug use. D.A.R.E. sends police officers into classrooms to teach students how to avoid drugs. The

Avoiding Drugs

officers role-play with students. They might say: "If someone tries to get you to smoke a marijuana cigarette, and you don't want to, what would you say?" Then they give examples of ways to say no without being embarrassed. This kind of practice can help when you are on the spot.

Think about what you would do if someone asked you to try drugs. Go over the situation in your own mind, or with friends. Being prepared for situations helps to handle them better. Thinking about something before it happens helps to figure out what to do when the situation actually comes up.

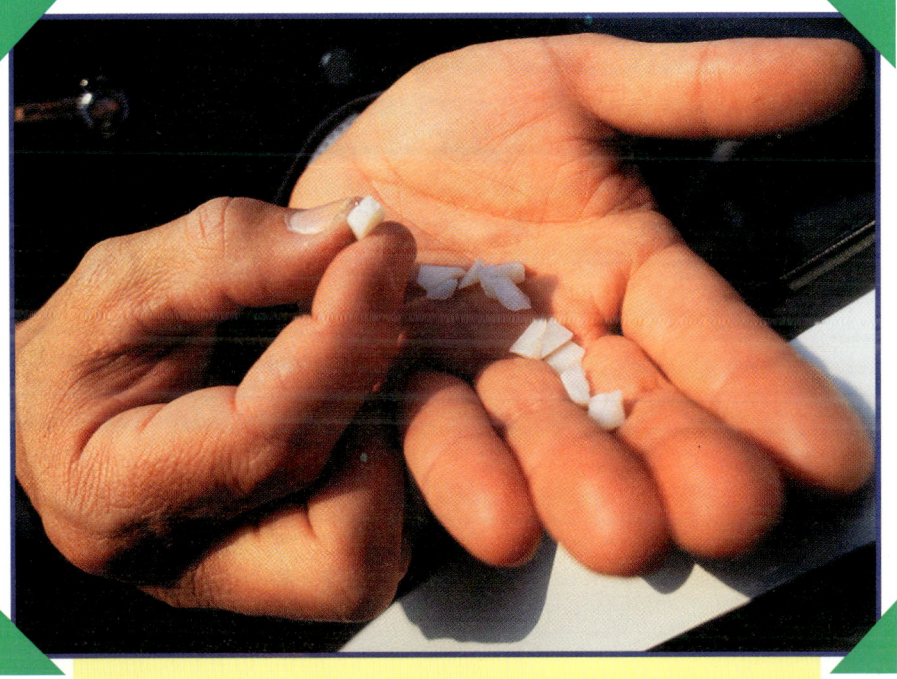

Drugs are all around. They are in schools and in neighborhoods. The accessibility of drugs may make saying no to them difficult. The consequences of drug use, however, can be severe.

Here are some answers you can use if someone asks you to smoke cigarettes, drink alcohol, or take drugs.

- I'm allergic to it.
- If my mother smells it on my clothes (or my breath) she will kill me.
- I'm not into that.
- If I get caught, I'll get kicked off the lacrosse (football, soccer) team.
- I hate the taste of beer.
- It makes me throw up.

Being prepared for situations helps to handle them. Practice saying no.

Do friends drink, smoke, or do drugs? Have they tried to get you to do these things too? If so, it might be a good time to make some new friends. It is no fun to be around kids who do things you are not interested in. Boredom is no excuse for hanging out with someone who does things that are not cool. There are lots of fun and exciting ways to fill time—for example, taking up a new sport.

Schools Helping Teens

Some schools teach drug education every day, just like math or science. One program, "The Science of HIV," is taught at many high schools across the country. It teaches students all about HIV, the virus that causes AIDS. Students learn that one of the easiest ways to get AIDS is by sharing needles used to do drugs such as methamphetamine or heroin. Participants learn how to protect themselves from HIV and AIDS by avoiding drugs.

Hackensack High School in New Jersey is one school that uses the program. Said principal Joe DeFalco, "The program has inspired a great deal of interest and concern among kids who think, 'It's not going to happen to me.'"[4]

In other communities, young people who have overcome their drug abuse share their experiences with their peers. Jaime, a former methamphetamine user, is in a special program to learn how to be a peer educator. The peer educators then go into school and tell other kids what really happens when someone abuses drugs. "Having real live kids talk to real live kids can be more effective than hearing grown-up speakers," Jaime said.[5]

What does Jaime tell kids about using drugs? "It's not worth it. . . . I did drugs, and I thought it was fun, but I never realized what I was giving up."[6]

One of the easiest ways to get AIDS is by sharing needles used to do drugs with an infected person. The quilt shown here remembers those who have died from AIDS.

Other Alternatives to Drug Use

There is so much bad news about drugs that sometimes it seems like everyone uses them. This just is not true. Millions of young people do not use drugs. Millions have never even been tempted to try them. The majority of young people do not even think of trying methamphetamine or any other drug as a way of feeling good. They have found other, healthier ways to have fun. Some of these things include:

- Playing sports on an organized team;
- Rollerblading, biking, hiking, or other sports you can do on your own;
- Singing or playing a musical instrument;

There are many activities and hobbies worth getting involved with instead of drugs. Hiking and backpacking, whether with friends or clubs, can be great fun.

Avoiding Drugs

- Mixing audio tapes for your friends;
- Earning money baby-sitting, dog walking, or doing other chores;
- Tutoring other kids;
- Doing volunteer work;
- Scouting or other after-school activities;
- Hobbies: for example, computers, acting, sewing, or drawing.

Doing something well builds self-esteem and produces a natural high. Feeling good comes from within, through learning new things and developing new interests.

There are many ways to have fun and feel good without drugs. Taking drugs is not worth risking your life. The best way to avoid getting hooked on methamphetamine or any other drug is never to try it.

chapter notes

Chapter 1. Methamphetamine—A Persistent Problem

1. Anastasia Toufexis, "There Is No Safe Speed," *Time*, January 8, 1996, <http://pathfinder.com/time/magazine/domestic/1996/960108/crime.htm> (May 25, 1998).

2. Steve Macko, "Methamphetamine Invades Middle America," ENN Emergency Services Report, April 13, 1997, <http://www.emergency.com/methinvd.htm> p. 1 (March 26, 1998).

3. Ibid.

4. Dirk Johnson, "Good People Go Bad in Iowa, and a Drug Is Being Blamed," *The New York Times*, February 22, 1996, p. 1.

5. Author telephone interview with Steve Johnson, Jasper County (Iowa) attorney, May 2, 1998.

6. Ibid.

7. Dirk Johnson, p. 1.

8. Macko, p. 2.

9. Author telephone interview with Michael Abrams, M.D., Director, Combined Medical Specialties, Broadlawn Medical Center, Des Moines, Iowa, June 9, 1998.

10. Carson Nightwine and Rowan Kelly, "Unabated Methamphetamine Abuses," *The Washington Times*, February 9, 1997, <http://www.ndcf.org/meth.html> (March 26, 1998).

11. Author telephone interview with Steve Johnson.

12. Ibid.

Chapter 2. About Methamphetamine

1. Carey Goldberg, "Way Out West and Under the Influence," *The New York Times*, March 16, 1997, p. 16.

2. Christopher S. Wren, "The Illegal Home Business: 'Speed' Manufacture," *The New York Times*, July 8, 1997, p. A8.

3. Anastasia Toufexis, "There Is No Safe Speed," *Time*, January 8, 1996, <http://pathfinder.com/time/magazine/domestic/1996/960108/crime.htm> (May 25, 1998).

4. Steve Macko, "Methamphetamine Invades Middle America," ENN Emergency Services Report, April 13, 1997, <http://www.emergency.com/methinvd.htm> p. 1 (March 26, 1998).

5. Christopher S. Wren, "Sharp Rise in Use of Methamphetamines Generates Concern," *The New York Times*, February 13, 1996, p. 16.

6. Ibid.

7. Carson Nightwine and Rowan Kelly, "Unabated Methamphetamine Abuses," *The Washington Times*, February 9, 1997, p. 21.

8. "Methamphetamine Abuse," *NIDA Capsules* (Bethesda, Md.: National Institute on Drug Abuse), p. 1.

9. Lloyd D. Johnston, Patrick M. O'Malley, and Jerald G. Bachman, *National Survey Results on Drug Use from the Monitoring the Future Study, 1975–1993*, vol. 1 (Rockville, Md.: National Institute on Drug Abuse, 1996), p. 121.

10. Carey Goldberg, "Way Out West and Under the Influence," *The New York Times*, March 16, 1997, p. 16.

11. Ibid.

12. Methamphetamine Fact Sheet, NCADI, Prevention Online, <http://www.health.org/pubs/qdocs/meth.htm> (March 26, 1998).

13. Ibid.

14. Dirk Johnson, "Good People Go Bad in Iowa, and a Drug is Being Blamed," *The New York Times*, February 22, 1996, p. 1.

15. Dan Egan, "Methamphetamine Abuse Contributes to Pair's Deaths," *Idaho Post Register*, <http://www.idahonews.com/news/local/methgirl.htm> (March 26, 1998).

16. Carey Goldberg, "Way Out West and Under the Influence," *The New York Times*, March 16, 1997, p. 16.

17. "President Signs Bill to Control Methamphetamine," October 4, 1996, <http://www.btg.com/uscm/US_Mayor_newspaper...11_to_Control_Methamphetamine_101696.html> (March 26, 1998).

18. Patrick Harrington, "To Control 'Meth,' Authorities Curb Cold Pills," *The Wall Street Journal*, August 25, 1998, p. B1.

Chapter 3. Using Methamphetamines

1. Krista Larson, "Girls Use Meth to Lose Weight," *Iowa Gazette*, GazetteOnline, <http://www.gazetteonline.com/health/hlth116.htm> (March 26, 1998).

2. Ibid.

3. Dan Egan, "Methamphetamine Abuse Contributes to Pair's Deaths," *Idaho News*, <http://www.idahonews.com/news/local/methgirl.htm> (March 26, 1998).

4. Becky Stover, "C.R. Students Hear Anti-Meth Message," *Iowa Gazette*, GazetteOnline, <http://www.gazetteonline.com/health/hlth116.htm> (March 26, 1998).

5. Jason DeParle, "Newest Challenge for Welfare: Helping the Hard-Core Jobless," *The New York Times*, November 20, 1997, p. A28.

6. Dirk Johnson, "Good People Go Bad in Iowa, and a Drug Is Being Blamed," *The New York Times*, February 22, 1996, p. 1.

7. "Judge Orders Woman to Visit Victim's Grave," *The New York Times*, October 11, 1998, p. 28.

Chapter 4. Where Methamphetamine Came From

1. *Methamphetamine Abuse: NIDA Capsules* (Bethesda, Md.: National Institute on Drug Abuse), p. 2.

2. Dirk Johnson, "Good People Go Bad in Iowa and a Drug Is Being Blamed," *The New York Times*, February 22, 1996, p. 1.

3. Methamphetamine Fact Sheet, p. 1, <http://www.lec.org/DrugSearch/Documents/Meth.html> (March 26, 1998).

4. Ibid.

5. Christopher S. Wren, "The Illegal Home Business: 'Speed' Manufacture," *The New York Times*, July 8, 1997, p. A8.

6. Ibid.

7. Ibid.

8. Christopher S. Wren, "Sharp Rise in Use of Methamphetamine Generates Concern," *The New York Times*, February 13, 1998, p. 16.

9. *Methamphetamine Abuse*, p. 2.

10. "What Is Crystal Methamphetamine?" Schick Chemical Dependency Program, <http://aaw.com/schick/crystal1.html> (March 26, 1998).

11. Alan I. Leshner, Ph.D., "Treatment: Effects on the Brain and Body," Speech Before the National Methamphetamine Drug Conference, May 28–30, 1997.

12. Ibid.

13. Wren, "Sharp Rise in Use of Methamphetamine Generates Concern," p. 16.

14. "Methamphetamine," <http://www.lec.org/DrugSearch/Documents/Meth.html> (March 26, 1998).

15. "What Is Crystal Methamphetamine?" Schick Chemical Dependency Program, <http://aaw.com/schick/crystal1/html>.

16. Methamphetamine Fact Sheet, <http://www.lec.org/DrugSearch/Documents/Meth.html>.

Chapter 5. Fighting Abuse

1. Author telephone interview with Steve Johnson, Jasper County (Iowa) attorney, May 2, 1998.

2. Author telephone interview with Michael Abrams, M.D., director, Combined Medical Specialties, Broadlawn Medical Center, Des Moines, Iowa, June 9, 1998.

3. Ibid.

4. Ibid.

5. Ibid.

6. Ibid.

7. Author telephone interview with Steve Johnson, May 2, 1998.

8. Author telephone interview with Michael Abrams, M.D., June 9, 1998.

9. Ibid.

10. Ibid.

Chapter 6. Avoiding Drugs

1. Carson Nightwine and Rowan Kelly, "Unabated Methamphetamine Abuses," *The Washington Times*, February 9, 1997, <http://www.ndcf.org/meth.html> (March 26, 1998).

2. Christopher S. Wren, "Survey Suggests Leveling Off in Use of Drugs by Students," *The New York Times*, December 21, 1997, p. 24.

3. "Survey Hints at Rise in Use of Hard Drugs by Preteens," *The Record* (Hackensack, N.J.), August 14, 1997, p. 11.

4. Patricia C. Turner, "HIV Course Has Good Science, Good Lessons," *The Star-Ledger* (Newark, N.J.), November 2, 1997, p. 27.

5. Steve Gravelle, "Blairstown Girl, 17, Testifies About Drug Use," *The Gazette*, <http://www.gazetteonline.com/news/9804/apr044.htm> (March 26, 1998).

6. Ibid.

where to write for help

D.A.R.E. America
P.O. Box 2090
Los Angeles, CA 90051-0090
(800) 223-DARE
<http://www.dareamerica.com>

National Clearinghouse for Drug Information
P.O. Box 345
Rockville, MD 20847-2345
(800) 729-6686
<http://www.health.org>

Parents Resource Institute on Drug Education (PRIDE)
3610 DeKalb Technical Parkway, #105
Atlanta, GA 30340
(770) 458-9900
<http://www.prideusa.org>

Phoenix House Foundation
164 W. Sixty-fourth Street
New York, NY 10023
(212) 595-5810

further reading

Condon, Judith. *The Pressure to Take Drugs.* New York: Franklin Watts, 1990.

Hurwitz, Sue, and Nancy Shneiderman. *Drugs & Your Friends.* New York: The Rosen Publishing Group, Inc., 1992.

Mass, Wendy. *Teen Drug Abuse.* New York: Lucent Books, 1997.

McFarland, Rhoda. *Drugs and Your Parents.* New York: The Rosen Publishing Group, Inc., 1991.

Methamphetamine & "Ice." York, Pa.: William Gladden Foundation, 1992.

Schleifer, Jay. *Methamphetamines.* Center City, Minn.: Hazeldon Foundation, 1998.

Internet Addresses

Drug Enforcement Agency
<http://www.usdoj.gov/dea/pubs>

Indiana Prevention Resource Center at Indiana University
<http://www.drugs.indiana.edu/prevention/meth.html>

National Institute on Drug Abuse
<http://www.nida.org/nih/gov>

index

A
Abrams, Dr. Michael, 8, 9, 37, 38, 45, 48, 49, 50
addiction, 40, 43, 44
 in babies, 21
adrenaline, 39, 41
AIDS, 54, 55

B
behavior, 19
bikers, 12, 34
brain, effects on, 49

C
central nervous system, 32, 39
Clinton, Bill, 21, 22, 51
Comprehensive Methamphetamine Control Act, 10, 51
Controlled Substances Act, 34
counseling, 48
crack cocaine, 37, 51
crank, 38
crimes, 21, 21, 29

D
D.A.R.E., 52
deaths, 14
dieting, 25, 26, 43
dopamine, 39, 41
Drug Abuse Warning Network (DAWN), 15, 51
Drug Enforcement Agency (DEA), 11, 12, 14, 39

E
effects, 40
environmental hazards, 21
ephedrine, 34

F
factories, use in, 8, 9
forms of methamphetamine, 36

H
Hackensack High School, 54
health hazards, 42
HIV, 54

I
ice, 38
ingredients, 36
injecting, 37

J
Johnson, Steve, 9, 44, 49

L
labs, 13, 14 ,22, 34

M
McCaffrey, Barry, 21
Mexican Connection, 11
Monitoring the Future Survey, 15
motorcycle gangs, 12, 34, 36

N
National Institute of Justice, 16
needle sharing, 42
nicknames, 12, 36

O
odor, 36

P
peer pressure, 24, 52
pollution, 21
pseudoephedrine, 35
puberty, 24

R
Reno, Janet, 39
Rolling Stones, 18
rush, 38

S
schizophrenia, 9
signs of abuse, 45
smoking, 37
snorting, 37
stages of abuse, 20
Superman syndrome, 19

T
therapeutic communities, 49
treatment, 47
tweaking, 19

U
use among young people, 15

W
Warner-Lambert, 23
weight loss, 17, 24, 33
White House Office of National Drug Control Policy, 14
withdrawal, 27
women users, 16
World War II, 32

Z
zero tolerance, 11